Pet Charms
Bunny Surprise

by Amy Edgar
illustrated by Jomike Tejido

SCHOLASTIC INC.

To Haya Sophia – J.T.

Library of Congress Cataloging-in-Publication Data

Names: Edgar, Amy, author. | Tejido, Jomike, illustrator. • Title: Bunny surprise / by Amy Edgar ;
illustrated by Jomike Tejido.Description: First edition. | New York : Scholastic Inc., 2017.
Series: Pet charms ; #2 | Summary: Molly has a magic charm bracelet that lets her understand
what animals are saying, so when she accompanies her friend to the pet store to pick out a pet, the
two rabbits tell her that they would like to stay together. • Identifiers: LCCN 2016030461 | ISBN
9781338045901 (pbk.) • Subjects: LCSH: Rabbits—Juvenile fiction. | Magic—Juvenile fiction.
Bracelets—Juvenile fiction. | Human-animal communication—Juvenile fiction. | CYAC: Rabbits—Fiction.
Magic—Fiction. | Bracelets—Fiction. | Human-animal communication—Fiction. Classification:
LCC PZ7.E225 Bu 2017 | DDC [E]—dc23 LC record available at https://lccn.loc.gov/2016030461

10 9 8 7 6 5 4 3 2 1   17 18 19 20 21

Printed in China
First edition, February 2017
Book design by Steve Ponzo

Molly had a magic bracelet.

When she wore it, she could understand animals.

No one knew her secret.

The bracelet glowed as she put it on.

Molly heard a knock.

It was Lexie, Molly's neighbor and best friend.

"Hi," said Molly. "Happy day before your birthday!"

"Thanks!" said Lexie.

Molly's cat, Stella, padded into the room.
Lexie petted her.
She had always wanted a pet of her own.

"Guess what," said Lexie.

"Mom said I could have a pet for my birthday!"

"That's super!" said Molly.

"What kind will you get?"

"I'm not sure," said Lexie.

"We don't have room for a cat or dog."

"That's okay," said Molly.

"There are <u>lots</u> of great pets."

"I know what we should do," said Molly.

"Let's go to Paws Palace."

"Great idea!" said Lexie.

"Your Aunt Vera knows all about animals."

The girls walked down the block.
Molly rang the bell.
"Hello, girls," said Aunt Vera.
"Come on in."

Molly spotted her good friend, Mr. Wiggles.
Molly had saved the puppy during a storm.
He had given her the magic bracelet.

Mr. Wiggles jumped into her arms.
"Hello, friend!" he barked.
He licked her face.

"What brings you girls here today?" asked Aunt Vera.

"Lexie wants to pick out a pet," said Molly.

"You have so many animal friends, Aunt Vera!" said Lexie.

"Look over here," said Molly.

A green snake smiled up at her.

"Pleassssssssssssed to ssssssssssee you," he hissed.

"Oh," said Lexie. "Look at the bunnies!"
Two bunnies stared back at the girls.
Aunt Vera handed each girl a bunny.

"This brown bunny is so sweet and soft," said Lexie. "I would love to have him for a pet."

"This one is sweet, too," said Molly.

The white bunny looked sad.
Molly leaned in.
She heard the bunnies talking to each other.
"Did you hear what that girl said?"
asked the white bunny.

"That she wants to take us home?"
asked the brown bunny.
"Yes, but only <u>one</u> of us," said the white bunny.
"Oh no!" cried the black bunny.
"But you are my best friend."

Molly bent down.

"Maybe I can help," she whispered.

"That would be great!" said the white bunny.

"Lexie, I think these bunnies are best friends," said Molly.

"Like us," added Lexie.

"I bet they want to stay together," said Molly.

"You may be right," said Aunt Vera.
"Most rabbits are happiest when they have a friend.
They keep each other company."

"Can they share one home?" asked Lexie.
"Yes, it's called a hutch," said Aunt Vera.
"So two bunnies take up the same amount
of room as one!" Molly added.

"Maybe I could adopt <u>both</u> bunnies," said Lexie.
Molly winked at the bunnies.
They wiggled their whiskers.

"Let's go talk to my mom," said Lexie.
She blew the bunnies a kiss.
The friends left Paws Palace.

Molly and Lexie ran to Lexie's house.
"How was your day, girls?" asked Lexie's mom.
"Super! We visited Paws Palace," said Molly.

I met two cute bunnies who need a home," Lexie said.

Great," said Lexie's mom.

Which one should live here?"

"Well, Mom, we learned a lot about bunnies," said Lexie. "Bunnies are happiest when they have a friend."

"Plus, two bunnies can share one hutch," said Molly.

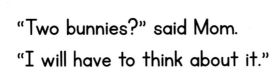

"Two bunnies?" said Mom.
"I will have to think about it."
Lexie turned to Molly.
"I can't wait for the pet surprise
at my party tomorrow!" she said.

Lexie's party was off to a great start.
She was opening presents.

Then the doorbell rang.

It was Aunt Vera – with the two bunnies.

"It's a bunny surprise!" shouted Molly.

"<u>Both</u> bunnies are for me?!" Lexie asked.

"Chocolate or vanilla?" asked Lexie's mom.

"Both, please," said Molly.

"Chocolate and vanilla go great together."

"Hey, that's what I'll name my bunnies!" said Lexie.

"Thank you for being our friend, Molly," said Vanilla.
Then Molly saw her bracelet sparkle brightly.
She blinked.
A new bunny charm was hanging from it!

Molly smiled at Chocolate and Vanilla.
She was happy to have two furry new friends!
Molly dug into her cake.